MORIAH

Dallas, Texas

A GIRL NAMED

MORIAH

Jerry W. Burns

Dedication

To the innocent children,

Of all races and colors.

May peace and love prevail.

Everyone has a story to tell.

And every story is important.

The long summer days stretched endlessly across the vast Delta country, a level horizon as far as the eye could see, the only relief being in the clouds hanging in the August sky.

The warm, quiet skies are decorated endlessly with huge puffy clouds which move slowly this time of year, forming the most amazing shapes. The silence of the landscape, good at times, could be almost unbearable, with nothing but endless rows of cotton.

Cotton, as far as a person could see, seemed almost a reflection of the puffy, white clouds against the Creator's canvas of blue sky. For a person born in the Delta country, the landscape is never ending. No hills, mountains, valleys or forests – only a few trees and the vast landscape of cotton.

This is low, lonesome country, almost as though no one lives here.

The little girl loved to lie in the soft, warm earth of the freshly hoed rows of cotton plants and gaze at those magnificent white clouds of August; for hours almost without end, the innocent little girl would look at the puffy white clouds as they moved across the dark blue canvas and see wondrous shapes in the form of human faces and animals in those clouds of summer.

Her name was Moriah and the animals and people in those clouds were her friends, the only friends she had. She discovered animals, and creatures that only a bright, imaginative child could understand and appreciate.

It was amazing that the little girl understood things that she had never seen before. But she was blessed with a vivid imagination, and intelligence that was not common.

The wonderful animals that Uncle told her about that lived on the other side of the great ocean stirred the imagination of the bright young child named Moriah.

The summer days stretched endlessly across the vast cotton fields of West Tennessee. Moriah had never seen anything else except those wonderful animals and faces; and the clouds.

Uncle had described the wonderful animals on the other side of the great ocean with tears forming and shining on his handsome, dark face. He told Moriah, about the lions and elephants and the other animals too numerous to mention, animals of his homeland that would never be seen again.

Uncle and all the older people would never be able to adjust to a new land, a new world, where they were strangers. With no chance to learn, they were condemned to forced solitude and inhumane work; and the constant humiliation of being treated like livestock or not even as well. They were forever denied their beliefs, customs, history, culture and humanity.

It is difficult to see those old cotton fields today and not be moved to despair over the cruelty that humans are possible of inflicting.

Moriah saw the wonderful creatures in the summer clouds and occasionally saw the great evil ship that Uncle told her about, the cruel ship that carried people in chains far from their homes never to be seen again.

Many times, at night, Uncle would close his eyes and softly hum, in a rich, deep voice, the chants and songs of his people heard and indelibly stamped on his memory during the many long miserable weeks of suffering in that inhumane dark hold of the old wooden ship. We simply cannot begin to imagine the pain, filth, disease, degradation, fear and horror of those cargo holds in the bottoms of the slave-trading ships. We must be reminded, less we forget. Uncle hummed those chords and melodies almost constantly.

Sometimes Uncle's eyes would be closed while he hummed for long periods of time in the tiny dark cabin in West Tennessee.

The sad, gentle man, trying to drive away the memory of the constant sound of chains and shackles beating against the massive wooden beams of the old ship, would hum softly at first – and then louder and louder, trying to drive away the memory which intruded into his rest from a long day in the cotton fields of the plantation.

Beads of perspiration covered his face and pulsating veins rose on the forehead of his handsome dark face. The song of utter despair coming from the rich baritone voice of the old slave would bring tears to the heart of anyone who is truly human.

Almost every night in the warm dark cabin, the old man's humming for long periods of time would finally put him to sleep, long after the little girl had already closed her eyes for the night.

The billowing summer clouds flowing across the rich, verdant Delta country were the only books Moriah knew. The imaginary animals and friends she saw each day in the clouds were the only source of images she had of people and animals.

The most important image that Moriah had, was that of her young, beautiful mother she would never see again. For many weeks after her mother was taken away Moriah cried, until one day she could cry no more. The little girl did not understand why her mother was taken away.

It happened one day when the neighboring plantation owner came by to visit Master and saw Moriah's mother. She was the most beautiful slave, he had ever seen, and he offered Master a bag of gold for the fair skinned young woman – Moriah's dear mother.

That day, as the carriage carried her mother into the dust of twilight, Moriah ran after the carriage, crying her heart out, until Master arrived on his thoroughbred horse to bring her back to the little cabin.

Moriah – cared for now by Uncle – cried many days and nights for her mother. Finally, she simply cried no more; there were no tears left. But Moriah did see her mother in the brooding clouds almost every day.

That was the end of any settled happiness for Moriah, who would never know freedom and carefree happiness. Moriah was only a child and beautiful, but she was a slave and would never be free. It's unimaginable in this great country that such cruel dominion over people could ever have been tolerated.

Moriah never had any playmates or even knew any other children. Often, she would see the little blond- haired girl in the fancy clothes at a distance, playing under the great sheltering oak tree. But she was forbidden to go close and meet the little girl in fancy clothes with books and play toys.

Moriah never had a toy except the tiny rag doll she found at the edge of the cotton field one day. She treasured the little doll and kept it hidden under a pile of rocks. She would only uncover the doll and play with it when she was certain no one else was around to see her.

Moriah knew she would be beaten and the doll taken away if anyone discovered her secret.

Toward the end of the summer in which her mother was taken away, Master and his family were away from the plantation for a few days and Moriah was pulled by wonder up the steep hill to the old oak tree where the little white girl played.

Along the way Moriah found a great treasure. It was a book with wonderful pictures and black marks. Moriah didn't even understand what a book was and that the black marks or words told a story.

By looking at the pictures – the first she had ever seen – Moriah was able to discover a wonderful story. All the images in the magic book were of white children.

Many days later as Moriah was looking intently at the pages of the little book, she was suddenly pushed over, and a tiny white hand grabbed the book. The little white girl shouted, "What are you doing with my book?" Moriah tried to explain that she found the book and meant no harm; she only wanted to look at the wonderful pictures.

Of course, the child of bondage had no words for "book" or "picture" in her limited vocabulary, even though she was very bright and quick to learn.

Master's little girl screamed in Moriah's face, "You don't know how to read, and slaves don't need books."

The little girl in the beautiful dress and shiny shoes took the book and ran to the oak tree and put the book in the knothole in the tree. Now the sources of pleasure and discovery for Moriah were greatly diminished.

For the child born in slavery there would never again be access to another book.

***

After the passing of several more summers Moriah became an attractive young woman, a carefree child of summer no longer. She was very pretty like her mother.

While Moriah was still in her early teens, she became a mother herself and named her daughter Priscilla.

Moriah and her daughter Priscilla lived in a tiny slave cabin on the immense cotton plantation with a gentle, sensitive, dark-skinned man, named Stephen.

Moriah often wondered which of the men on the plantation – who had their way with her – was the father of her child.

Priscilla, like her mother and grandmother, was fair skinned and attractive, but she was a slave with no voice of protest or refusal.

Sixteen years remained before the abolition of slavery and the end of the dark, bloodied and horrible war that divided our people – fought in the streets, cities and farms of our young nation.

***

The year was 1849, when Master wrote and recorded his last will and testament. Born in 1773, he was the son of a captain in the Revolutionary War, the grandson of a Virginia doctor and the owner of a large cotton plantation in West Tennessee, at the edge of the rich and fertile Delta country.

The following is from his last will and testament:

I... Give to my wife during her natural life my man, Stephen, my woman Moriah and her child Priscilla...

***

The old wooden, three-mast, slave-trading ship, fighting a deadly storm midway across the vast, cold Atlantic, climbs a steep mountain sized wave and suddenly dives and slams into the ocean trough below in the darkness of midnight.

The chains and iron shackles binding the dark-skinned humans clang and rattle relentlessly.

The moans of hundreds of humans, packed side-by-side into the dark, hot, disease – ridden cargo hold, like sardines in a tin container, waft upward to the salty air on the deck where the slave ship owner and captain listens, his soul haunted by the ancient tribal melody filtering through the unceasing moans and chants, telling of human bondage, suffering and despair.

Years later, that same Captain, John Newton, could not forget the evil slave trade of his past and those constant moans and ancient chants. John Newton became increasingly distraught over his former life, finally becoming an active Christian and writing, quite possibly, the greatest Christian hymn of all time, to the melody of those haunting moans and ancient African chants.

Amazing grace, how sweet the sound, that saved a wretch like me!

I once was lost, but now am found, was blind, but now I see.

I pray that one by one, beautiful voices will join with Uncle, all across the South from the blue ridges of Virginia, down through the Smoky Mountains of the southern Appalachians, down into valleys and ancient hollows, across vast open fields and into dismal swamps along the Delta, to the Gulf; from tiny slave cabins on the ridges, in valleys, deserts, forests, and along great rivers, and the songs of suffering and despair will still be heard from a great chorus – 10 million souls who were hunted, captured and chained like animals; who moaned a haunting song of bondage in the sinful holds of the slave – trading ships.

***

This story is written to honor the memory of Moriah, Stephen and Priscilla, family members. They now rest in peace with generations of family beneath that huge oak tree on a sunny hillside in West Tennessee.

***

If you have taken time to read this story, I ask you to join with me in prayer that we may be forgiven the sins of racism and hatred. May we be united people, never again in our country to hold another human in bondage. Please join in our effort to fight all forms of human slavery and human trafficking, including the sex trade and pornography. Pray for the innocent little children. Protect them.

Thank you,

Jerry W. Burns

Jerry W. Burns

Lives in Dallas, Texas where he has a son and daughter and they each have a son and daughter. Jerry studied philosophy at the University of Michigan and graduated from Abilene Christian University.

Jerry is an author, artist, craftsman, and skilled photographer. He has been a pilot, sports car racer, broadcaster, pastor, yacht designer and manufacturer. He was Vice President of Burns Manufacturing, builders of Burns-Craft houseboats, cruisers, and motor yachts.

www.ingramcontent.com/pod-product-compliance
Lightning Source LLC
Chambersburg PA
CBHW071229130626
46555CB00004B/1915